MISFIT ACADEMY: SEMESTER 3

R.L. WILSON

Copyright © 2024 by R.L. Wilson All rights reserved.

No parts of this book reproduced or transmitted in any form or by any means, electronically or mechanically, including photocopying, recording, or by any information storage and retrieval system without permission in writing from the publisher.

This is a work of fiction names characters, businesses, places, events, and incidents are either the products of the authors imagination or used in a fictious manner. Any resemblance to actual person living or dead or actual events is purely coincidental.

Warning: The unauthorized reproduction or distribution of this copyrighted work is illegal. Criminal copyright infringement, including infringement without monetary gain, is investigated by the FBI and is punishable by up to 5 years in prison and a fine of $250,000.

Cover Designer: Exquisite Premades

Editing: Rainlyt editing

Proof Reader: Cassie Hess-Dean

Formatting: R.L. Wilson

R.L.Wilson Misfit Academy Semester 3, The Paige Storm Series Book 2 October 2024 R. L.Wilson/Exquisite Novelty Publishing LLC

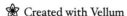 Created with Vellum

Thank you for purchasing Misfit Academy 3
Thank you to all my supporters, friends, Arc group, and beta readers for encouraging me, even on the days when I wanted to throw the towel in.
Special thanks to my many mentors. Your mentorship is invaluable. You kept me motivated, gave me advice, and never asked for anything in return. The world needs more people like you.

Special thanks to my husband and kids who stayed up late listening to my ideas and being alpha readers. I hope to make you guys proud of me.

Last but not Least I have to thank God for giving me the strength and the courage to keep striving.

R.L. Wilson

FREE BOOK

Signup for my newsletter and claim your free book.
 https://dl.bookfunnel.com/loqjdqjg4o

Check out my website
 www.rlwilsonauthor.com

BLURB

Time travel is messy. And when my roommate is lost somewhere in the timeline, it gets even worse.

Simon's missing, and it's all my fault. I've been bouncing through centuries like I'm on some kind of magical rollercoaster, trying to find him. But when I finally discover a wooden device that helps me control where I go, Prentiss—the vampire nightmare I can't seem to shake—steals it. And he's not alone. He's teamed up with a tall, creepy guy from the Chronomancers, and together they want to rewrite time itself.

Now, I have no way of pinpointing Simon, and every leap through time feels like a gamble. If I can't get the device back, not only will I lose Simon for good, but Prentiss and his new ally could change the past—and future—in ways I can't even imagine.

Time's running out, and this time, I can't afford to lose.

This is an upper YA/NA Slow burn Academy Romance with no need to choose. The steaminess increases throughout the series.

AUTHOR NOTE

I feel compelled to say that this is a **Slow-burn Academy RH romance.** If you love all the delicious tension of a budding relationship. And want to be practically screaming for it when they finally get it on, this book is for you.

If you are looking for a steamy, kinky book with lots of sex. Please **reconsider reading this book.** I don't want to disappoint readers, you will be disappointed if you are looking for tons of sex. This is an adventure the sex will come eventually...

You've been warned. If you are still here for it. Please read on.

Cheers,
R.L. Wilson

CHAPTER ONE

Frightened? Yes, that was an understatement. I was practically shaking as I squeezed Jake's hand tightly. The flickering fluorescent lights and the hum of outdated technology created a disorienting backdrop. I was determined to find Simon—our group was like family and abandoning him to the fog of the 1990s was unthinkable.

We pushed our way through the crowded hallways of the old school, which now seemed like a bizarre amalgamation of my own time and a bygone era. The students around us were decked out in garish neon colors, their hairstyles sporting enough volume and hairspray to defy gravity. Their stares, curious and hostile, followed us as we navigated the corridors. Each glance felt like a sharp reminder of just how out of place we are.

"Let's go," Jake urged, his grip on my hand firm and reassuring. He tugged me along, his voice a steady beacon amidst the chaos. We moved with purpose, weaving through clusters of students who looked at us with a mix of confusion and mild irritation. It felt like we were trapped in a time capsule, surrounded by the relics of a decade that was not our own.

My heart raced as we approached the cafeteria. It was a gamble, but Simon's insatiable appetite for snacks and food could lead us to him. If he was anywhere, he was probably here, navigating through a sea of cheesy nachos and sodas.

As we pushed open the heavy cafeteria doors, the scent of stale pizza and overcooked vegetables hit us. The room was a cacophony of noise—students chatting, trays clattering, and the occasional burst of laughter. My eyes scanned the room frantically, searching for a familiar face.

"Where do you think he'd be?" Jake's voice was strained, his gaze sweeping across the room. "Do you think he'd be at a table, or maybe in line for food?"

Before I could answer, my gaze landed on a figure moving purposefully toward the back exit. He was tall and striking, with a handsome, brown-skinned face that seemed to radiate confidence. But what caught my eye was the wooden device clutched tightly in his hand—the very artifact we've been chasing.

"There!" I hissed, pointing toward him. Jake's eyes followed my gesture, and his expression shifts to one of "I got you sucka."

The man's presence was magnetic, his stride quick as he headed toward a side door, likely aiming to escape. Without hesitation, Jake and I darted toward him, dodging through the maze of cafeteria tables and trays.

"Hey!" I called out, my voice catching in the noisy chaos. "Stop!"

The man's head snapped in our direction, his eyes widening slightly with recognition. It was clear that he realized we were onto him. With a swift motion, he turned and bolted for the door, the wooden device swinging with him.

"Damn it!" Jake cursed under his breath. "He's getting away!"

We sprinted after him, our footsteps echoing through the hallways as we closed in on the man. I could see his panic-stricken face as he reached the exit and yanked the door open, disappearing into the brisk 1990s air outside.

"Jake, we have to catch him!" I shouted, but my voice was nearly lost in the roar of our pursuit. We burst through the door, the cold air hitting us like a slap.

The man was running across the school grounds, heading toward the edge of the campus. I could see him glancing back, his pace faltering slightly as he realized we were gaining on him. The urgency in his movements was palpable, his attempts to flee growing increasingly desperate.

"Get the device!" I urged Jake, who was closing the gap between us. "We need it!"

With a final burst of speed, Jake lunged for the man, tackling him to the ground. The struggle was intense, the man writhing beneath Jake's firm grip. I could see the wooden device skittering away, the small but crucial object tumbling across the grass.

I scrambled for the device, my fingers fumbling in the grass. Just as I reached it, the man managed to wrench free from Jake's grasp and bolted toward the edge of the campus. I saw Jake's face tighten with frustration but quickly focus on the device.

Clutching it to my chest, I called out to Jake, "We've got it! Let's get back to school!"

Jake hesitated only a moment before scrambling to his feet and running back toward the school with me. Our breath formed clouds in the chilly air as we raced through the corridors, the panic of our encounter still fresh in our minds.

Back inside, we found a quiet corner in an empty classroom where we could catch our breath. I fumbled with the device, trying to figure out how to use it. Jake stood close by, his eyes scanning the classroom as if expecting the man to burst through the doors at any moment.

"We need to get out of here," Jake said, his voice taut with urgency.

I nodded, focusing on the device. "We can't leave Simon" spills from my lips. A quick breeze swept across me and I took Jake's hand, and together we prepared for the jump back to our own time.

"Ready?" I asked, glancing at Jake's determined face.

"Ready," he replied, gripping my hand tightly.

The world around us blurred and spun as we were pulled through the vortex of time. The familiar hum of magical energy surrounded us, and the sensation of being pulled through space and time is both exhilarating and terrifying.

With a sudden jolt, we found ourselves back on campus, and the comforting familiarity of the present time enveloped us. My heart raced with a mixture of relief and anxiety. We'd made it back, but Jake was still missing, and we needed to figure out how to bring him home.

As we stood there, catching our breath, I felt the weight of the device in my hand. The quest was far from over, and the stakes were higher than ever. We had to find Simon and bring him back before it was too late.

CHAPTER TWO

My heart raced with a mixture of anticipation and nervous energy as I adjusted the strap of my leather satchel. Tonight felt different—like the air was charged with something more than just magical energy. My fingertips brushed the edge of the wooden device nestled within, a relic we'd uncovered from the shadowy depths of a stranger. It was supposed to be a key to bending time, but its secrets were still locked away.

Dana and Jake chit chatted as we made our way down the dimly lit hallway of the school. Dana's fiery auburn hair cascaded down her back, catching the occasional flicker of torchlight, and her eyes sparkled with the kind of knowing that came from her psychic abilities. Jake walked beside her. His presence was almost magnetic. He had this intense energy about him—like a storm barely contained. I couldn't help but feel a pang of longing whenever I glanced at him.

Our destination was Nathaniel's dorm room, which was tucked away in a quieter part of the academy. I admired Nathaniel's calm magic and his gift for unraveling magical mysteries. If anyone could help us unlock the potential of the device, it was him.

The dorm grew quieter as we approached Nathaniel's door, the usual hum of magical activity fading into the background. I knocked, my hand trembling slightly with excitement. Jake's presence beside me was grounding, a comforting reminder that I wasn't alone in this.

"Come in!" Nathaniel's voice called out, smooth and resonant, carrying with it a hint of curiosity.

I pushed the door open and led the way into Nathaniel's room. His space was a treasure of ancient tomes, mystical artifacts, and glowing orbs. It was exactly as I had imagined—a sanctuary for someone who lived on the edge of magical knowledge. Nathaniel was at his cluttered desk, his fingers tracing runes on a parchment. When he looked up, his dark eyes sparkled with recognition and interest.

"Ah, Paige, Dana, Jake—what a pleasant surprise," he said, rising with an effortless grace. His robes rustled softly as he approached. "I assume you're here for more than just a casual chat."

I nodded, feeling a surge of determination. "Yes, we need your help with this." I carefully placed the wooden device on his desk, watching as his eyes widened with intrigue.

Nathaniel examined the artifact closely, his fingers brushing over the intricate carvings. "This is quite remarkable," he murmured. "Where did you find it?"

"In the old library archives," Dana answered, stepping forward. Her hands glowed faintly, a sign of her psychic prowess. "We think it has the power to manipulate time, but we can't figure out how to use it.

Luckily, Dana was able to think quickly on her toes. There was no way could we tell Nathaniel where we really found it. He would only scorn me for time traveling.

Nathaniel's expression grew thoughtful. "It appears to be an ancient time-traveling artifact.

The carvings suggest it involves complex temporal magic and elemental forces."

Jake, leaning casually against the doorframe, watched with curiosity and a clear protective edge. His presence was both reassuring and distracting. My heart fluttered every time I glanced at him, and I fought to keep my focus on Nathaniel and the device.

"How does it work?" I asked, my voice tinged with both hope and frustration.

Nathaniel's gaze shifted to the glowing orbs on his desk, and he began to sort through them. "Time travel requires more than just magic; it needs precise control over temporal currents. This device will need to be attuned to a specific time and place. We'll need to perform rituals and align it with temporal energies."

My heart leaped at the thought of finally understanding how it worked. "What do we need to do?"

Nathaniel's eyes sparkled with enthusiasm as he started preparing the ritual space. "First, we need to determine the exact time and place you want to visit. Once we have that information, we'll synchronize the device with those coordinates."

Jake stepped closer, his eyes meeting mine

with a depth of understanding that made my pulse quicken. "How can we avoid getting lost in time?"

Nathaniel's reassuring smile eased some of my tension. "Careful preparation and protective spells will guide you. I'll ensure the device is properly attuned. But remember, time travel is inherently risky. Be prepared for the unexpected."

Dana's eyes glowed brighter as she tapped into her psychic abilities. She had obviously sensed the challenges we might face and added, "What about astral alignment? Will that be necessary?"

"Absolutely," Nathaniel confirmed. "Aligning with the astral currents will be crucial. Dana, your abilities will be essential in this process."

As Nathaniel continued preparing, I felt a flutter of anxiety mixed with excitement. Jake's warmth beside me was a constant comfort. His presence was grounding, especially as we faced the unknown together. I stole a glance at him, feeling a mix of love and apprehension.

Nathaniel arranged the orbs and drew arcane symbols on the floor with meticulous precision. Dana's glowing hands wove a protective light around the room, creating a shimmering barrier. The air was thick with magical energy, each movement charged with purpose.

Jake leaned in, his voice a soft murmur against the crackling energy. "No matter what happens, we'll face it together."

His words wrapped around me like a warm embrace, grounding me in the moment. "Together," I echoed, my voice filled with resolve.

With everything in place, Nathaniel stepped back, his eyes reflecting the focused determination I felt surging through me. "Are you ready?"

The room fell silent, save for the soft hum of the protective wards. The wooden device began to glow softly, resonating with the ritual's energy. As the protective barrier enveloped us, I took a deep breath, feeling both the weight of the moment and the thrill of the journey ahead.

With Nathaniel's guidance, we were about to embark on a voyage through time—one that would test our courage, our love, and our understanding of everything we knew. No matter what, we had to find Jake. I dared not tell anyone we lost him in time. Everyone already thought I cursed Randy.

CHAPTER THREE

The swirling vortex of energy consumed us, and the world around us dissolved into a whirlpool of colors and sensations. I clutched the wooden device tightly, my heart racing as the time travel spell took hold. Beside me, Dana's grip was ironclad on my arm, her breath coming in rapid, frightened puffs. Jake, the anchor, kept a steady hand on my shoulder, his warm presence a comforting shield against the chaos.

"Hold on!" Jake's voice was barely audible over the roar of the magical storm that enveloped us. The sensation of being pulled through time was disorienting, a rush of cold and heat, light and dark. My stomach lurched with each twisting second.

Suddenly, the maelstrom ceased. We stumbled out onto a snow-covered landscape, our feet crunching into the thick, powdery snow. The cold hit us like a sledgehammer, numbing my fingers and cheeks instantly. I looked around, trying to orient myself, but the vast, snowy expanse made it difficult. Snow-clad mountains loomed in every direction; their peaks lost in a swirling mist.

Dana shivered violently next to me, her eyes wide with fear. "Where are we?" she asked, her voice trembling as she clung to me. Jake, too, was scanning the surroundings, his breath visible in the freezing air.

I pulled out my phone, though the cold air made it difficult to operate the screen. The picture of Simon, the one we'd been using to track him, was displayed prominently. We needed to find him—and fast. But first, we needed shelter. Without coats or any sort of protection from the biting cold, we were at the mercy of the elements.

"Let's find somewhere warm," I said, my teeth chattering despite my best efforts to stay composed. The snow was falling harder now, and the cold was seeping into my bones. "We need to find a place to ask about Jake and get out of this weather."

We trudged through the snow, the cold air making every step feel like an ordeal. The landscape was stark, with no sign of civilization except for distant figures bundled in large coats moving purposefully through the snow. They didn't seem to notice us—or if they did, they chose to ignore the three shivering strangers in their midst.

After what felt like hours of stumbling through the snow, our breath clouding in front of us, we spotted a small, dimly lit cabin nestled among the snow-covered trees. The sight was both a relief and a beacon of hope. We made our way towards it, our footsteps slowing as we neared.

The door of the cabin creaked open before we could knock. A brown-skinned man with a broad, kind face and dark eyes stood in the doorway. His expression shifted from surprise to concern as he took in our frozen forms.

"Come in quickly!" he said, his voice warm and welcoming despite the chill outside. We shuffled inside, the warmth of the cabin enveloping us like a cozy blanket. I could hardly believe how good it felt, the heat immediately thawing my frozen fingers.

We glanced around the room—a simple, rustic interior with wooden furniture, a roaring fireplace, and shelves lined with various trinkets and books. It was a stark contrast to the icy world outside.

"Thank you," I said, still shivering as I fumbled to show him Simon's picture. "We're looking for someone. His name is Simon. Have you seen him?"

The man took the phone, studying the image with a furrowed brow. "I'm afraid I haven't seen anyone who matches this description. I haven't had many visitors recently."

Before I could respond, the peaceful atmosphere was shattered by a low rumbling sound. The cabin trembled, and I could hear the distant roar of what sounded like an avalanche. Panic surged through me, and I exchanged frantic glances with Dana and Jake.

"We need to leave—now!" Jake shouted over the growing noise. His face was reddened with fear, I supposed.

I grabbed the wooden device from my satchel, my hands shaking as I fumbled with it. The rumbling was growing louder, the very ground beneath us shaking with the force of the approaching avalanche. Snow seeped into the cabin through the cracks, and the warmth we had just begun to enjoy was rapidly disappearing.

The man's face went pale as he glanced outside, his eyes wide with alarm. "You must go! The avalanche is coming!"

In a flurry of desperate action, we clustered around the wooden device. I activated it with trembling hands, my mind racing to remember the incantation Nathaniel had taught us. The device began to hum as the air crackled with temporal energy.

"We've got to get out of here!" Dana's voice was almost lost in the roar of the avalanche, her eyes wide with terror. She clung to Jake and me as the cabin was rocked by the force of the rumbling.

As the first snowflakes began to drift into the cabin, I whispered a silent prayer, hoping the device would work. The air shimmered around us, the world beginning to blur and distort. The avalanche's roar was deafening, and I felt the biting cold return as the warmth of the cabin began to fade.

This device might take you to the right year

but it damn sure doesn't take you to the right place.

We were enveloped in a swirl of energy once more, the world shifting around us. My heart pounded in my chest as we were pulled away from the imminent danger. The last image I saw was the man's worried face and the encroaching wall of snow.

In the final moment before everything dissolved into the swirling vortex of time, I glanced at Jake and Dana. Our eyes met, filled with a shared fear. We had escaped one danger, but what awaited us next was unknown, and the icy chill of the avalanche had left a lingering dread.

As the world spun around us, I could only hope that wherever we ended up, it would be safer than the snow-covered nightmare we had just fled.

CHAPTER FOUR

The warmth of the campus was a stark contrast to the icy wasteland we had barely escaped. As soon as we materialized back in the academy's familiar haven, a profound sense of relief washed over me. Jake, Dana, and I had barely spoken since our return; the harrowing experience in the snow had left us shaken, and we were all eager for the comforting familiarity of our home.

"Next time, let's avoid the avalanches, okay?" Jake's voice was a low rumble as he brushed snow from his shirt, but the tension in his tone was unmistakable.

Dana nodded in agreement, her expression one of deep concern. "We need a better plan. That was too close."

The wooden device lay heavy in my satchel, its secrets still tantalizingly out of reach. I placed my satchel in the closet on the back shelf for safe keeping. It was both a burden and a beacon of hope. As much as the experience had terrified me, I couldn't bring myself to part with it. The stakes were too high, and Simon's fate too uncertain.

The next day, I went to class, hoping that normalcy would help me forget the chilling terror of the previous night. I lost myself in lectures and notes, trying to push away the lingering fear and the image of the avalanche roaring towards us. The normal rhythm of academic life was a welcome distraction, but the device's weight remained a constant reminder of the unknown dangers that still awaited us.

As the last bell rang and students began to filter out of the classroom, I packed up my things and slipped them into the safety of my satchel. I took a deep breath, steeling myself for the rest of the day. The hallways were busy, bustling with students eager to get to their next classes or lunch. I tried to blend into the crowd, but a prickle of unease began to settle at the back of my mind.

It was then that I saw him—a man standing

in the corridor, his presence like a shadow falling over the bright, noisy atmosphere. He was tall, with an unkempt appearance and a menacing aura that made my stomach twist with anxiety. His clothes were old-fashioned, almost as if he had stepped out of another era entirely. His eyes locked onto me with an intensity that made my skin crawl.

"Paige Storm," he called out, his voice a harsh rasp that cut through the noise of the hallway. "I know you have it. Hand it over."

My heart skipped a beat. How did he know my name? And what was it that he wanted? My grip tightened around the strap of my satchel. .

"Excuse me?" I tried to keep my voice steady, but the tremor in my voice betrayed my fear. I turned to walk away, hoping that if I ignored him, he would lose interest.

But he was faster than I anticipated. Before I could react, he had grabbed my arm with a vice-like grip. His touch was icy, sending a jolt of panic through me. I could feel the raw, electric energy emanating from his skin, crackling and snapping as it made contact with mine.

I gasped as an intense, searing pain shot through my arm, like lightning coursing through my veins. The electricity surged up my arm, radiating a burning sensation that made me cry out in pain. The man recoiled; his face contorted in agony. He moaned loudly, his hands clutching at his own body as if he had been struck by a sudden, debilitating shock.

In the chaos, I yanked my arm free, the pain still lingering as I staggered backward. The man's eyes, wide with pain and anger, followed me as I stumbled away. His mouth moved in silent fury, his hands still twitching as he tried to shake off the effects of whatever had happened.

I didn't wait to see what he would do next. My heart pounded in my chest, adrenaline fueling my flight as I turned and ran. The hallways blurred around me, students scattering out of my path as I barreled down the hallway, my breath coming in ragged gasps.

"Paige!" Dana's voice reached me through the haze of panic. I turned just in time to see her and Jake hurrying towards me, their faces etched with concern. They must have seen my frantic escape and come to my aid.

I didn't stop to explain. Without a word, I surged past them, my focus solely on reaching the safety of our dorm. The man's presence was still a haunting shadow in my mind, his ominous threat lingering even as I left him behind. Every step felt like an eternity as I raced towards the familiar, comforting walls of our living quarters.

Behind me, the sound of footsteps and muffled voices grew fainter, and I dared to glance back. The man was no longer in sight, but the unsettling feeling of being pursued remained. My mind was a whirlwind of fear and confusion. Who was he? How did he know about the device? And why had his touch felt like a jolt of pure, raw electricity?

Finally, I burst into the dormitory. The door slammed shut behind me with a satisfying thud. I leaned against it, my breath coming in ragged gasps as I tried to calm my racing heart. Jake and Dana were right behind me, their faces a mix of worry and urgency.

"What happened?" Dana asked, her voice a soothing balm against the chaos of my thoughts.

"There was a man—he knew about the device. He tried to take it from me," I explained, my voice trembling as I recounted the encounter. "When he touched me, there was this surge of electricity. It hurt so much..."

Jake's eyes were dark with concern. "We need to figure out who he is and why he's after you. And we need to be ready—he might come back."

I nodded, my mind racing with possibilities. The encounter had left me shaken, but it also strengthened my resolve. We couldn't let fear paralyze us. The device was too important, and whatever secrets it held were worth fighting for.

As I clutched the wooden device tightly in my hands, I knew that our journey was far from over. If anything, it had just begun. The danger was real, and the stakes were higher than ever. We needed to find out more about this mysterious man and his connection to the time-traveling artifact.

For now, I had to stay vigilant, for the past and the future were intertwined in ways I had yet to fully understand. And as I glanced around the safety of our dorm room, I couldn't shake the feeling that the storm was far from over.

CHAPTER FIVE

The library was eerily quiet, the only sounds the soft rustle of pages and the occasional whisper of a turning book. I loved this place; it was our sanctuary. But today it felt more like a crypt, holding secrets we desperately needed to uncover. Jake, Dana, and I had set up camp at one of the old wooden tables near the back, surrounded by stacks of ancient texts and dusty tomes.

Jake's brow was furrowed in concentration as he pored over a particularly old volume. Dana, seated beside him, was muttering softly under her breath, her fingers tracing patterns in the air as she used her psychic abilities to sift through the magical wards and illusions protecting the library's more sensitive materials.

"I still can't believe he knew about the device," Dana said, her voice barely a whisper. "How is that even possible?"

I glanced at Jake, who was squinting at the faded text of a leather-bound book. "I don't know, but it's clear we're dealing with something bigger than we thought. If this secret organization is as powerful as it seems, we need to know everything about them."

The book Jake was reading had strange symbols and ancient writing that looked like a mix of runes and archaic script. "This is a history of magical artifacts," he said, flipping through the pages. "But it doesn't mention the device specifically. Maybe we need to look into organizations that might be interested in time-traveling technology."

I nodded and pulled out the wooden device from my satchel, setting it carefully on the table. Its polished surface gleamed under the soft library lights. The device had become a symbol of our quest, its intricate carvings and enigmatic power both a blessing and a burden.

"I'll check the archives," I said, determination lacing my voice. "The older records might hold some clues about this secret organization."

Dana and Jake exchanged a glance but

nodded in agreement. I stood up and made my way to the archives, a labyrinthine section of the library filled with ancient scrolls, manuscripts, and artifacts. The air here was thick with dust and the faint scent of old parchment.

The archives were hidden behind a heavy oak door, which creaked open with a groan as I entered. Rows of shelves lined the walls, each filled with neatly organized records. I began scanning through the files, looking for anything related to secret organizations or time-traveling artifacts.

As I pulled out a particularly ancient-looking scroll, a sudden chill ran down my spine. I glanced around, feeling a prickling sensation of being watched. The air seemed to grow colder, and the shadows in the room lengthened. I shook off the feeling and focused on the task at hand.

Hours seemed to pass in a blur. I poured over documents, each one revealing a piece of the puzzle. Then, I stumbled upon a hidden compartment behind a false wall. Inside, I found a collection of old manuscripts bound in dark leather. My heart raced as I pulled one out. Its cover was embossed with a symbol I recognized from the book Jake had been reading: an intertwined serpent and hourglass.

With trembling hands, I unwrapped the manuscript and began to read. The text was written in a combination of old magic script and a language I could barely decipher. I took a deep breath and concentrated, using my own magical knowledge to translate the key passages.

The manuscript spoke of a clandestine group known as the "Chronomancers." According to the text, they were an ancient organization dedicated to controlling time and preserving magical artifacts with the potential to alter history. Their methods were ruthless, and their influence stretched across different eras. The device we had, with its power to manipulate time, was exactly the kind of artifact they would seek to control.

I flipped through the pages, my eyes widening as I read about their rituals and practices. The Chronomancers were not only interested in acquiring artifacts but also in harnessing their power for their own purposes. The manuscript detailed their methods for tracking and acquiring these objects, revealing a network of informants and operatives who scoured different periods for such valuable items.

My heart pounded as I realized the implications. The man who attacked us must be one of their operatives, and if he was after the device, it meant the Chronomancers were closer than we thought.

I hurried back to the main table, where Jake and Dana were still working. "I found something," I said, trying to keep my voice steady. "It looks like we're dealing with an organization called the Chronomancers. They have a history of seeking out time-traveling artifacts, and they're known for being extremely dangerous."

Jake looked up from his book, his eyes narrowing. "The name sounds familiar. I think I read something about them in the book I was looking at. But it didn't go into detail."

Dana's eyes widened. "This makes sense. If they've been operating in the shadows for centuries, it would explain why they knew about the device and why they're so determined to get it."

I nodded, feeling a surge of anxiety mixed with determination. "We need to find out more about them—who their leaders are, where their base of operations might be, and how we can stop them from getting their hands on the device."

Jake stood up, his face set with resolve. "We should start by looking into any recent activities or sightings of Chronomancers. If they're active now, there might be some clues in more recent records."

Dana agreed, her expression focused. "I can use my psychic abilities to see if there are any lingering impressions or magical traces that might lead us to their current activities."

We gathered our findings and made our way back to our usual study area, setting up our notes and research materials. The weight of what we had learned hung heavily over us. The Chronomancers were a formidable enemy, and our quest to protect the device had just become even more urgent.

As we worked, I couldn't shake the feeling that we were standing on the precipice of something much larger than ourselves. The Chronomancers were not just a threat to us but to the fabric of time itself. We had to be prepared for whatever came next.

The library, once a haven, now felt like a battleground where we would face the shadows of the past and present. The time-traveling device, which had seemed like an intriguing artifact, had become the key to a perilous game of cat and mouse. And as the hours ticked by, I knew that the real battle was only just beginning.

CHAPTER SIX

I stood in front of the mirror, a smile tugging at my lips as I admired my reflection. Tonight was the Thanksgiving sock hop, and for the first time in a while, I felt like I was just another student, ready to enjoy a normal, festive evening. My dress was a deep, midnight blue with twinkling sequins that caught the light with every movement. My hair fell in soft waves around my shoulders. I gave myself one last look, whispering, "You look good."

Feeling a surge of confidence, I grabbed my shawl and headed out of the dorm room. The hallway was abuzz with excitement and the occasional burst of laughter as students prepared for the evening's festivities. The

Thanksgiving sock hop was a beloved tradition at the academy—a time when the usually intense atmosphere lightened up with dance, music, and celebration.

I made my way to Nathaniel's dorm room, a sense of anticipation fluttering in my chest. Nathaniel had been a comforting presence during our recent encounters, and there was an undeniable chemistry between us. Tonight, I hoped to enjoy the evening and share a dance or two with him,

Nathaniel's dorm room door was slightly ajar, and I knocked softly before pushing it open. Inside, the room was filled with the warm glow of fairy lights and the soft hum of music from a vintage radio. Nathaniel was adjusting his bow tie in front of a small mirror, his expression a mix of concentration and amusement.

"Hey," I said, stepping in. "Ready for the sock hop?"

He looked up and smiled, his eyes lighting up when he saw me. "Paige, you look stunning. Come in, let me see you properly."

I twirled for him, the skirt of my dress flaring out in a playful dance. "Thanks! I'm excited. It's been a while since I've been to a school dance."

Nathaniel's eyes lingered on me for a moment longer than necessary, and then he offered me his arm with a grin. "Shall we?"

We walked together toward the main hall, where the sock hop was in full swing. The room was decorated with garlands of autumn leaves and strings of fairy lights that made everything look enchanted. The floor was filled with students in retro attire, dancing to a mix of classic tunes and lively beats.

As we entered the room, Nathaniel led me to the center of the dance floor. The music changed to a slow, melodic tune, and he pulled me close. We danced together, swaying gently to the rhythm. His touch was warm, his hand resting comfortably on my waist.

"You know," Nathaniel said, his voice low and intimate, "I've been meaning to talk to you about something."

I looked up at him, my curiosity piqued. "What's up?"

"I heard about the strange man who tried to take the device from you," he said, his tone serious. "It's concerning. I've been thinking... maybe you should stop time traveling for a while. It's too dangerous, and the Chronomancers, they're a real threat."

My heart sank at his words. "I can't just stop. We have to find Jake and make sure the device doesn't fall into the wrong hands. There's too much at stake."

Nathaniel's grip on me tightened slightly, his concern evident. "I understand that, Paige. But you have to be careful. The more you use the device, the more you risk drawing their attention. I don't want you to get hurt."

I looked into his eyes, seeing the genuine worry there. "I promise I'll be careful. But I can't just sit around and do nothing."

He sighed, his expression softening. "Okay. Just promise me you'll be cautious. And if you need any help, you know where to find me."

We continued to dance, the conversation drifting to lighter topics as we enjoyed the evening. The warmth of his presence and the rhythm of the music made me feel more at ease, if only for a few hours.

After a while, I excused myself to get a drink. The refreshment table was laden with all sorts of festive treats, from cranberry punch to pumpkin pie. As I reached for a glass of punch, I noticed a boy at a nearby table, his hair a striking shade of red that stood out even in the bustling room.

He was sitting alone, his gaze fixed intently on me. There was something about him—an odd mixture of urgency and curiosity—that made me pause. He was signaling for me to come over, his hand gesturing with a subtle but insistent motion.

I hesitated and glanced back at Nathaniel, who was chatting with some friends near the dance floor. My curiosity got the better of me, and I approached the red-haired boy, weaving through the crowd.

"Hi," I said as I reached his table, my voice tinged with curiosity. "You wanted to see me?"

The boy looked up, his eyes an intense green that seemed to pierce through the dim light of the room. "I've been waiting for you," he said in a low, urgent voice. "I know who you are and why you're here."

My heart raced. "And who exactly are you?"

He glanced around as if to make sure we weren't overheard. "My name is Rian. I have information about the Chronomancers. But we don't have much time."

My pulse quickened, a mix of apprehension and excitement swirling within me. "What do you know?"

Rian's gaze was earnest, his voice barely

above a whisper. "They're closing in on you. I've seen their plans, and they're more dangerous than you can imagine. You need to know what's coming before it's too late."

Before I could ask more, Rian's expression shifted, and he looked around nervously. "We need to talk somewhere more private. Can you meet me later? I'll explain everything."

I nodded, feeling a knot of unease settle in my stomach. "Sure. Where?"

Rian's eyes flickered with a mix of relief and urgency. "There's a secluded garden behind the dorms. Meet me there in twenty minutes."

He gave me one last fleeting, intense look before rising from his seat and melting into the crowd. My mind raced as I made my way back to Nathaniel, my thoughts already spinning with the implications of Rian's cryptic message.

As I returned to Nathaniel's side, I felt the weight of the evening's revelations pressing down on me. The sock hop, which had started as a simple escape from our troubles, had taken a dark turn. Rian's warning was a stark reminder that the dangers we faced were far from over.

Nathaniel looked at me with a mixture of concern and fear. "Everything okay?"

I forced a smile, trying to push aside the

unease. "Yeah, just a bit of intrigue. But nothing we can't handle."

As we continued to dance, my thoughts were a whirl of uncertainty and anticipation. The night was far from over, and the mysteries of the Chronomancers were just beginning to unfold.

CHAPTER SEVEN

Hell no, I wasn't going by myself—been there, done that. The idea of confronting Rian alone sent shivers tumbling down my spine. The stakes were too high, and the risks too great. At the very least, I was taking Dana with me. I knew Nathaniel and Jake would never approve, but I wasn't about to let their worries sideline me. We had bigger fish to fry, and besides, they'd only try to keep me from meeting Rian. They wouldn't understand the urgency.

I found Dana near the refreshment table, helping herself to a slice of pumpkin pie. Her curly hair was pinned back with festive clips, and she looked every bit the part of a student enjoying a holiday dance. But I knew better;

Dana's intuition was sharper than most, and I needed her on my side tonight.

"Dana, I need a favor," I said, grabbing her arm and steering her away from the crowd. "I need you to come with me. There's someone I need to meet. He says he has information about the Chronomancers and their connection to the time-traveling device. We need to check it out. It's too risky to go alone."

She raised an eyebrow but nodded. "Alright, I'm in. But this better be worth it. The sock hop was supposed to be a break from all the madness."

I couldn't help but smile at her grudging acceptance. "It will be. I promise."

We left the dance behind, slipping out through a side door and making our way across the chilly campus grounds. The night air was crisp and smelled of fallen leaves, a stark contrast to the warmth and festivity of the sock hop. The garden behind the dorms was a secluded spot, a place few students ventured to after dark.

"Are you sure about this?" Dana asked as we walked, her eyes scanning the shadows. "What if this is a trap?"

"I don't think it is," I said, though I couldn't

entirely shake my own unease. "Rian seemed genuine. Besides, he mentioned knowing about the Chronomancers. That's something we need to understand."

We reached the garden, a serene expanse of neatly trimmed hedges and ornamental statues. The moonlight cast an eerie glow over the space, and I could see a faint silhouette waiting near a stone bench. Rian's red hair was unmistakable, a fiery beacon in the darkness.

"Rian!" I called out softly as we approached. "We're here."

He turned, his green eyes catching the moonlight and reflecting an intensity that made me shiver. "You came. Good. I was worried you might change your mind."

Dana and I exchanged a glance, and I stepped forward, determined to get answers. "You said you have information about the Chronomancers and their connection to the device. What can you tell us?"

Rian nodded; his expression serious. "I'm a former student of the academy. I've been tracking the Chronomancers for years. They've been active since long before your time, and they have a deep interest in artifacts like the one you have."

I felt a rush of relief mixed with apprehension. "So, you know who they are? What they want?"

Rian took a deep breath, his gaze shifting between Dana and me. "The Chronomancers are a secret organization with a history dating back centuries. They are obsessed with controlling time and altering history to fit their own agenda. They've managed to stay hidden by using a network of spies and operatives. Their goal is to harness the power of time-traveling artifacts to manipulate events to their favor."

I glanced at Dana, who looked just as intrigued and concerned as I felt. "And what about Prentiss Darby? Do you know him?"

Rian's face darkened. "Prentiss is one of their leaders. He's a vampire who has been seeking powerful artifacts for centuries. He's particularly interested in the time-traveling device because it could give him unprecedented power. He eyes darted around. Especially if he can get his last life back. He's dangerous and ruthless, and he's been after you for a while."

My heart raced. "You mean Prentiss is the vampire who's been trying to get the device from us?"

Rian nodded grimly. "Yes. He's been using

his influence to gather information and resources. If he gets his hands on the device, it could mean disaster not just for you, but for the entire timeline."

Dana shivered beside me. "So, what do we do? How can we stop them?"

Rian took a step closer, his expression earnest. "I have some knowledge and skills that might help. I've studied their methods and learned about their hidden safehouses. We can use this information to our advantage. But I need your help to fully understand their plans and prevent them from succeeding."

I looked at Rian, weighing his offer. "What's your angle? Why are you helping us?"

Rian's gaze softened. "I have my own reasons. The Chronomancers took something very dear to me years ago, and I've been seeking justice ever since. Helping you aligns with my own goals, and it's a chance to finally put a stop to their manipulations."

Dana crossed her arms, her eyes narrowing. "And how do we know we can trust you?"

Rian's face was serious. "You'll have to take that leap of faith. But I promise you, I have no intention of deceiving you. I've been working alone for too long, and having allies could make a significant difference."

I glanced at Dana, who gave me a subtle nod. "Alright. We'll work with you. But you need to be upfront with us. No secrets."

Rian's expression was one of relief. "Fair enough. I'll provide you with what I know and help you navigate their operations. We have to move quickly—the Chronomancers are closing in."

As we spoke, I felt a new resolve settling in. The dance had been a brief escape, but the reality of our situation had returned with a vengeance. Rian's offer of help was both a glimmer of hope and a reminder of the dangers that lay ahead.

As we left the garden and headed back toward the dorms, the weight of our new alliance and the looming threat of the Chronomancers filled my thoughts. The night was far from over, and the path forward was fraught with uncertainty. But with Rian's insights, we had a chance to turn the tide. And for the first time in a long while, I felt like we might actually have a fighting chance.

CHAPTER EIGHT

The library had been our refuge for hours. Dana and I had poured over ancient texts and manuscripts, trying to uncover any scrap of information that might give us an edge against the Chronomancers. The dim light from our desk lamp cast flickering shadows, and the silence of the room was punctuated only by the soft rustling of pages and the occasional muttered frustration.

"Why does it always come down to ancient texts and forgotten prophecies?" Dana muttered, her eyes scanning the faded script of an old tome.

I sighed, rubbing my eyes. "Because the answers are often buried in the past. We just have to dig them up."

Jake, his brow furrowed in concentration, was flipping through a particularly old grimoire. "I think I've found something," he announced, his voice tinged with excitement. "It's a prophecy that sounds eerily similar to what we've been dealing with."

Dana and I leaned in, our curiosity piqued. Jake pointed to a passage that made my pulse quicken. The prophecy spoke of a device with the power to bend time and reality—the potential to either save or doom countless lives.

Dana's face turned serious. "So, this prophecy suggests that the device could alter history in catastrophic ways if it falls into the wrong hands."

I nodded, the cold realization settling in. "And Prentiss, the vampire after us, is mentioned in the prophecy. He's a key figure in this dark scheme."

Jake continued to read; his expression grim. "The prophecy describes someone who will seek the device to fulfill a dark purpose. It's a figure who has lived for centuries and manipulates events from the shadows. Sounds like Prentiss."

Dana shivered beside me. "We're up against

something much bigger than just a secret organization. We need to figure out what Prentiss plans to do with the device and how we can stop him."

Jake closed the book with a resigned sigh. "We've got a lot of work ahead of us, but at least we have a clearer picture now."

As we gathered our things, I felt a new wave of urgency. The prophecy had given us a glimpse of the potential catastrophe we faced, but we still needed more concrete information.

We made our way back to the dorms, and as I walked down the dimly lit hallway, a small book left outside my door caught my eye. I nearly tripped over it, my heart skipping a beat. I bent down and picked it up, noticing the old, leather-bound cover and the faint glow of its enchantment.

"Hey, is that another book?" Dana asked, her curiosity piqued.

"I think so," I said, examining the book. "It was just left here."

I slipped it into my book bag and turned to Dana. "We need to head over to your dorm. We've got to go over this before class. There might be something important in here."

Dana nodded; her expression serious. "Let's go."

We made our way to Dana's dorm, the early morning chill cutting through our hurried steps. The campus was still quiet, and the faint sounds of students stirring for the day could be heard in the distance. The book's weight in my bag felt like a beacon of hope—or a potential burden.

When we reached Dana's dorm, we quickly settled into her room. The familiar surroundings offered a momentary sense of comfort. I pulled the book from my bag and set it on her desk.

"It looks old," Dana remarked, her eyes widening with curiosity. "Do you think it's related to what we're dealing with?"

"I hope so," I said, opening the book carefully. The pages were yellowed with age, and the text was written in a script that was both intricate and ancient.

As I began to read, Dana leaned in, her eyes scanning the words alongside mine. The text spoke of a device with the power to alter reality. Its history was intertwined with dark forces and ancient prophecies. My heart raced as I realized that the book contained information that might be crucial to understanding the full extent of the threat we faced.

"Look at this," I said, pointing to a passage that described a ritual to harness the device's power. "This could be what Prentiss and the Chronomancers are trying to achieve."

Dana's eyes widened. "If they succeed in performing this ritual, they could rewrite history. We have to stop them."

The gravity of our situation was sinking in again. The book had provided more details about the prophecy and the potential catastrophic consequences if the device fell into the wrong hands. But there was still so much we didn't know.

"We need to find out more about the Chronomancers' plans," I said, closing the book. "And we need to figure out where Prentiss is and what he's planning."

As we finished our examination of the book, the reality of our situation became even clearer. We were facing a monumental threat, and time was slipping through our fingers. We had to act quickly and decisively.

We headed to class, the weight of our

discoveries and the urgency of our mission pressing heavily on us. The campus buzzed with the usual morning activity, but I couldn't shake the feeling that we were racing against an unseen clock.

As we walked across campus, my thoughts were consumed with the implications of the prophecy and the new information we had uncovered. The sense of dread and anticipation was almost overwhelming, but I knew we had no choice but to press on.

In the distance, I noticed a familiar figure standing near the entrance to the library—Rian. His red hair stood out against the backdrop of the campus, and his anxious expression told me he had more to share.

"Rian!" I called out, my voice cutting through the morning air.

He turned, his face a mixture of relief and urgency. "I've been looking for you. I've found more information about the Chronomancers and their plans."

I felt a surge of hope. "We've just uncovered a prophecy that ties into everything we're dealing with. Let's discuss it—there's a lot at stake."

As we gathered around a nearby bench, the

weight of the prophecy and the new information filled the air. The danger was far from over, and the path ahead was fraught with uncertainty. But with Rian's help and our newfound knowledge, we had a fighting chance. At least I hoped so.

CHAPTER NINE

The air in the common room of Dana's dorm was thick with the hum of late-night energy. Rian and Dana were deep in conversation, their voices low and teasing as they exchanged stories and shared laughs. The tension between them was palpable, each glance and playful remark hinting at a deeper connection. I watched from the side, a small smile tugging at my lips as I sipped on a cup of tea.

Dana's laughter rang out as Rian made a particularly amusing comment. "You're really good at this, you know," Dana said, her eyes sparkling with amusement.

Rian grinned, leaning closer. "I've had plenty

of practice. Besides, you're an excellent audience. It's easy to be charming when you have someone so easy to please."

Dana's cheeks flushed, and she leaned into him, her smile softening. "Oh, stop. You're making me blush."

I cleared my throat, my voice light to break the intimate moment. "Alright, you two, as much as I'm enjoying the flirt-fest, we have to get some sleep. We've got class in the morning and a lot of work to do."

Rian chuckled and stood up, offering Dana a hand to help her off the couch. "She's right. We've been at this for hours. Let's get some rest and regroup tomorrow."

Dana took Rian's hand, and their fingers lingered just a moment longer than necessary. I noticed the small, almost imperceptible smiles they exchanged, and the way Rian's gaze softened as he looked at her. It was clear they were both enjoying each other's company more than either of them were willing to admit.

I felt a pang of envy, but I pushed it aside. Dana deserved this—she was an amazing person and she needed moments of happiness amid all the chaos. Rian seemed like a good guy, and maybe, just maybe, they would find something special together.

After saying my goodbyes, I headed back to my own dorm. The campus was eerily quiet, the usual hustle and bustle replaced by a calm that felt almost too serene. I slipped into the elevator, the metallic doors closing with a soft thud behind me. As the elevator ascended, I let out a weary sigh, looking forward to a few hours of much-needed sleep.

When the elevator doors opened on my floor, I noticed something immediately—a faint, unsettling gap in the otherwise familiar view of the hallway. The door to my suite was ajar, a sliver of darkness peeking through the crack. My heart skipped a beat. It could be nothing, just a careless mistake, but a nagging sense of dread clung to me.

I stopped in my tracks, my mind flashing back to the last time my door had been left open. Randy had been lying on the floor, frozen by a dark magic. The memory was sharp, the fear and anxiety of that moment still fresh. I took a deep breath, steeling myself as I approached the door with caution.

"Simon?" I called out softly, hoping for a

reassuring response. There was no answer, only the silence of the empty hallway.

I eased the door open with a gentle push. The squeak of the hinges was loud in the stillness. My senses were on high alert as I stepped into the suite. Everything seemed in order at first glance—the living area was tidy, the kitchen immaculate. But the sense of unease only deepened as I approached my room.

When I reached my door, my breath caught in my throat. The door was slightly ajar, just like the suite's door, but the scene inside was far from reassuring. My room was in complete disarray. The once neatly arranged furniture was now scattered, clothes were strewn across the floor, and drawers hung open with their contents spilling out.

My heart raced as I stepped further inside, my eyes scanning the chaos. It took only a moment to realize that the wooden device—the time-traveling artifact—was missing. The spot where I had carefully hidden it was empty. The absence of the device struck like a blow to my gut.

"No," I whispered, my voice trembling. I had to be wrong. I had to be imagining things. But no matter how much I willed it to be otherwise, the device was gone. I rushed to the spot where I had last seen it, my fingers tracing the empty space where it had been secured.

Panic set in, my thoughts racing as I tried to piece together what had happened. Had someone broken in? Was Prentiss involved? My mind was a whirlwind of questions and fears, each one more unsettling than the last.

I pulled out my phone, hands shaking as I dialed Dana's number. The line rang, and I could hear the soft crackle of static on the other end.

"Hello?" Dana's voice was groggy, the sounds of her getting out of bed evident.

"It's me," I said quickly, trying to keep my voice steady. "Something's happened. The device—it's gone."

There was a stunned silence on the other end. "What? Paige, are you sure?"

"I'm positive," I said, my voice breaking slightly. "My room's been ransacked, and the device is missing. You need to get over here right now."

"On our way," Dana replied, her voice sharp with urgency. "Stay where you are. Don't touch anything."

I ended the call and took a deep breath,

forcing myself to remain calm despite the rising tide of anxiety. I moved away from the mess in my room, not wanting to disturb any potential evidence. I tried to think through the chaos, wondering who could have done this and what their next move might be.

Minutes felt like hours as I waited for Dana and Rian to arrive. The silence of the suite was oppressive, each creak of the floorboards or gust of wind outside amplifying the tension in the room. My thoughts were a jumble of fear and frustration, each passing second heightening the urgency of our situation.

When Dana and Rian finally burst through the door, their expressions were a mixture of concern and determination. Dana's eyes widened at the sight of the ransacked room, and Rian's face turned grim.

"This is bad," Rian said, stepping inside and surveying the damage. "We need to figure out what happened and how they found out about the device."

Dana crouched beside me, her face set in a hard line. "We need to alert the academy's security and figure out our next steps. This isn't just a burglary—it's a targeted attack."

I nodded, feeling the weight of our predicament settling heavily on my shoulders. The device was not just a powerful artifact—it was the key to our fight against the Chronomancers. Without it, our efforts were severely compromised.

CHAPTER TEN

The air in the hallway was cold and still as we made our way to Jake's room. The weight of the missing device pressed heavily on my shoulders, and I could feel the tension vibrating through me and Dana. We strutted in near silence, our minds swirling with a thousand thoughts and possibilities.

Jake was sitting on his bed, his eyes widening with concern as we entered. "What's wrong?" he asked, his voice tinged with worry.

"Paige's room was ransacked," Dana said, her tone clipped and urgent. "And the time-traveling device is gone."

Jake's expression darkened as he took in the news. "Damn it," he muttered, running a hand through his hair. "That's serious. We need to alert the authorities or—"

"Actually, we need to talk to Mr. Shank," I interrupted, cutting off his suggestion. "He's the only one who might understand the full implications of what's happened. But—" I hesitated, glancing at Dana, "—he's also warned me about meddling with the timeline. I'm not sure how he'll react."

Jake's eyes narrowed. "Mr. Shank? You're right. If anyone can help us understand the full extent of this mess, it's him. But if he's already warned you..."

"We need to take that risk," Dana said firmly. "If the device is gone, we don't have the luxury of second-guessing."

Reluctantly, I nodded. "Alright. Let's go."

We made our way across campus, the early morning fog shrouding the grounds in an eerie haze. The gravity of our situation made every step feel heavier, each breath more labored. When we reached the building where Mr. Shank's classroom was located, I felt a pang of apprehension.

Mr. Shank was known for his stern demeanor and strict rules about time travel. His warnings about the dangers of tampering with the timeline had always felt like a distant concern, but now they loomed large. I pushed open the door to his classroom, the sound of creaking hinges cutting through the silence.

Mr. Shank was at his desk, preparing materials for his next class. He looked up as we entered, his expression shifting from curiosity to alarm when he saw our faces.

"What's going on?" he asked, his tone sharp and demanding.

I took a deep breath, stepping forward. "Mr. Shank, we have a serious problem. The time-traveling device has been stolen."

His face went pale, and he stumbled slightly, clutching the edge of his desk for support. "Stolen? The device... but that's—"

I rushed to explain, trying to convey the urgency of the situation. "We don't know who took it or why, but we found my room ransacked and the device missing. We're afraid that whoever has it might use it for something dangerous."

Mr. Shank's expression turned grave as he sank into his chair, his face a mask of distress. "This is much worse than I feared. The device is not just a powerful artifact—it's a key to manipulating the very fabric of time itself. If it falls into the wrong hands..."

Dana stepped closer; her voice urgent. "What does this mean, Mr. Shank? How dangerous is this?"

Mr. Shank closed his eyes for a moment, taking a deep breath before speaking. "The device's power is immense. It can alter events in ways that might seem minor but can have catastrophic ripple effects through history. Even a small change can lead to unpredictable and often devastating consequences."

My heart raced as I listened to his words. "So, if the device is misused..."

"It could unravel the timeline," Mr. Shank said, his voice heavy with dread. "It could create paradoxes, distort history, or even collapse entire timelines. The balance of reality itself is at risk."

Jake's face was a mask of concern. "How did this happen? Why wasn't the device better protected?"

Mr. Shank shook his head. "The device was stored securely, but its power attracts attention. And if someone knew where to look or had the means to breach the security..."

I felt a wave of guilt wash over me. "I never

meant for this to happen. I was trying to understand the device better, to use it responsibly. Now—"

"No," Mr. Shank interrupted, his voice firm but not unkind. "You mustn't blame yourself. The responsibility lies with those who sought to misuse the device. But we need to act quickly. The longer the device is in the wrong hands, the more damage it can do."

Jake stepped forward; his expression resolute. "What do we do now? How do we track it down and prevent any damage?"

Mr. Shank took a deep breath, visibly regaining his composure. "We'll need to gather all the information we can about the device's last known location and its potential uses. We'll also have to work with the magical security team and possibly consult with other experts who understand the intricacies of time magic."

He looked at me with concern. "Paige, you need to stay involved. Your knowledge of the device will be crucial in understanding where it might be and what it could be used for."

I nodded, swallowing hard. "I understand. We'll do whatever it takes to get it back and prevent any harm."

Mr. Shank's gaze softened slightly, though

the worry in his eyes remained. "Be cautious. The device's theft could mean that someone is planning something very dangerous. We need to be vigilant and prepared for anything."

As we left Mr. Shank's classroom, the weight of his words settled heavily in my gut. The device was more than just a powerful artifact—it was a key to a potentially apocalyptic scenario. With every step, the urgency of our mission pressed down on us.

Jake, Dana, and I walked in tense silence, each lost in our thoughts. The campus was slowly coming to life as the first light of dawn touched the buildings. We had a new purpose now, but the path ahead was fraught with peril.

"We need to get organized," Dana said, breaking the silence. "We have to coordinate with the magical security team and dig deeper into the connections between the device and the Chronomancers."

"Agreed," Jake added. "And we need to stay on high alert. Whoever took the device is likely to make an appearance."

CHAPTER ELEVEN

The morning bell rang, its shrill clang echoing through the hallways and signaling the start of classes. I barely heard it, my mind preoccupied with the overwhelming weight of our recent discoveries and the urgency of retrieving the stolen device. Dana and I had barely had time to strategize before heading to our respective classes.

I was hurrying down the corridor, lost in thought, when a sudden commotion disrupted my focus. Students around me were moving erratically, their expressions a mix of confusion and terror. The once-familiar environment was transforming into a chaotic scene.

"What's happening?" I shouted, grabbing Jake's arm as he joined me in the hallway. His eyes were wide with panic, and he looked around frantically, trying to make sense of the chaos.

Before Jake could respond, the ground beneath us seemed to ripple. Students began to float off the ground, their screams of terror filling the air as they were propelled uncontrollably through the hallway. Books and papers swirled in a frenetic whirlwind, and the very fabric of reality seemed to warp and twist around us.

"Paige! Jake!" Dana's voice cut through the din, her figure emerging from the chaos. She grabbed my arm tightly. "We need to find cover!"

As we struggled to stay grounded, I saw him. Prentiss, the vampire who had been lurking in the shadows, appeared at the end of the hallway, his eyes gleaming with a malevolent glow. Beside him stood the tall man—the one who had attacked me and nearly taken the device.

The sight of them together was chilling. They moved with a predatory grace, their presence amplifying the chaotic energy around us. It was clear they were responsible for the time distortions. The hallway seemed to buckle and twist as if it were a living entity under their control.

"Time is unraveling." Prentiss's voice was a low, ominous rumble. "And it's all thanks to your meddling, Paige."

I tried to steady myself, my heart racing as the room continued to destabilize. "You're going to pay for what you've done!"

With a sudden, powerful surge, the two villains launched themselves at us. The tall man—whose name I still didn't know—lashed out with dark energy, sending a burst of shadowy tendrils toward us. I ducked, pulling Jake out of the way as the tendrils collided with the wall, leaving scorch marks and causing a shower of sparks.

Dana retaliated with a shield spell, her hands glowing with a protective aura. The shield deflected the dark energy, but the sheer force of the attack sent her stumbling back. Jake shifted into his wolf form, his powerful muscles tensing as he prepared to defend us. His growls echoed through the hallway, mingling with the cacophony of the distorted environment.

Prentiss's eyes burned with a cold fury. "You

think you can stop us? This is only the beginning."

The entire hallway seemed to be in a state of flux. Walls rippled and warped, and the ceiling above us began to twist and stretch, distorting reality. Students continued to float uncontrollably, their screams merging into a horrifying symphony of chaos.

I grabbed Jake's arm, trying to pull him toward a corner where the distortion seemed less intense. "We need to get out of here!" I shouted over the noise.

But as we moved, Prentiss's shadowy form blocked our path. He raised his hand, and a surge of dark energy shot toward us. I barely managed to conjure a protective barrier in time. The force of the blast sent me crashing into the wall. Pain exploded across my body as I crumpled to the ground, my vision blurring.

"Paige!" Jake's anguished cry pierced through the chaos. He lunged toward me, but before he could reach me, the tall man appeared beside him, striking with a powerful burst of energy. Jake was thrown back, landing with a painful thud.

I struggled to get up, my limbs trembling with exhaustion and fear. Dana was engaged in a fierce battle with the tall man, her spells crackling through the air in a desperate attempt to hold him off. The hallway continued to distort around us, each second stretching into an eternity as time itself seemed to falter.

In the midst of the chaos, I saw a familiar face—Nathaniel. He appeared at the entrance of the hallway, his expression one of grim determination. His eyes locked onto Prentiss and the tall man, and he immediately took action.

"Get away from them!" Nathaniel shouted, his voice carrying a commanding authority that cut through the turmoil. He raised his hands, a powerful wave of energy erupting from his position and sweeping through the hallway.

The wave of energy collided with Prentiss and the tall man, pushing them back and disrupting their control over the distortion. The intensity of Nathaniel's spell momentarily stabilized the area, the floating students and swirling debris falling back to the ground.

But the respite was short-lived. Prentiss and the tall man recovered quickly, their expressions darkening with rage. Nathaniel's presence had clearly angered them, and their next moves were swift and violent.

Nathaniel's eyes met mine across the

chaotic battlefield, his expression conveying both urgency and concern. "Paige, you need to get out of here! Find somewhere safe!"

The hallway buckled once again, and the distortion intensified. Nathaniel was locked in a fierce confrontation with Prentiss and the tall man, his powerful spells clashing against their dark magic. The environment continued to warp and twist, the stability we had briefly regained slipping away.

I looked at Jake and Dana, both of them battered and struggling to stay on their feet. "We have to move!" I shouted. "Now!"

As we made a desperate attempt to escape the collapsing hallway, I could feel the ground shifting beneath me, the walls closing in. Nathaniel's spell continued to hold off the attackers, but the strain was evident on his face. His struggle was our only hope to escape.

The hallway seemed to stretch endlessly, each step feeling like a battle against an invisible force. The chaos around us was almost unbearable, but with Nathaniel's help, we managed to reach a safer area, away from the immediate danger.

Breathing heavily, I glanced back toward the hallway, where Nathaniel was still fighting fiercely. The sound of clashing magic and the crackling energy filled the air, a stark reminder of the danger we faced.

The battle raged on, and the cliffhanger of our situation was clear. We had escaped the immediate danger, but the fight was far from over. Nathaniel's presence had given us a brief reprieve.

As we huddled together, watching the chaotic scene unfold from a safer vantage point, I knew that the fight for the device and the stability of our world was far from over. The battle was raging, and the outcome remained uncertain.

CHAPTER TWELVE

The closet was cramped, but at least it offered some semblance of refuge from the madness that was unfolding outside. Dana, Jake, and I huddled together. The sound of the chaotic battle reverberated through the walls. The distant thrum of magical energy and the occasional crash of spell collisions were a constant reminder of the danger just beyond our hiding spot.

Jake's face was set in a grim expression, his fingers twitching as if itching to join the fray. I could see the determination in his eyes, and I knew he was wrestling with the decision that lay before him.

"I can't stay here," Jake finally said, his voice low and resolute. "I have to help Nathaniel."

My heart sank. "Jake, it's too dangerous out there. We don't even know what's going on."

"I know," he interrupted, "but he needs all the help he can get. And if I don't go, I might not be able to help at all." He gave me a reassuring look that didn't quite reach his eyes. "You two stay hidden. I'll find a way to turn the tide."

Before I could protest further, Jake was already moving toward the closet door. Dana and I exchanged worried glances as he pushed the door open and stepped into the corridor. The hallway beyond was illuminated in unsettling hues of red and orange, casting long, distorted shadows that danced on the walls.

"Be careful!" I called out after him, my voice muffled by the tight space.

Dana and I listened as Jake's footsteps echoed faintly, growing fainter as he ventured further into the chaos. I wished more than anything that I could follow him, but staying hidden was our only option for now. The intensity of the battle outside was far beyond anything I had ever faced, and every instinct told me to stay put.

Suddenly, a loud, piercing sound erupted from the corridor—a cacophony of magical energies clashing and exploding. My heart raced as I listened to the sounds of combat intensify. Dana and I pressed ourselves closer together, trying to block out the noise and the fear that gnawed at us.

Minutes felt like hours, and the tension in the closet was nearly unbearable. I was just starting to wonder how long we'd have to wait when we heard it—a deep, rumbling crash that reverberated through the building. The sound was deafening, shaking the walls and sending tremors through the floor.

"What was that?" Dana whispered; her voice tight with fear.

"I don't know," I replied, my mind racing. "But it can't be good."

We exchanged another glance, both of us knowing that staying hidden wasn't an option forever. We had to find out what was happening. Slowly, Dana and I emerged from the closet, our hearts pounding in our chests.

As we stepped into the hall, we were greeted by a scene of destruction. The hallway was littered with debris, and the walls were scorched and cracked. The red glow that had earlier illuminated the space now pulsed ominously, casting an eerie light over everything.

In the midst of the chaos stood a door at the far end of the hall, glowing a fierce, angry red. It was clear that it was magically warded—an impenetrable barrier that seemed to pulse with an otherworldly energy.

"What is that?" Dana asked, her eyes wide with concern.

"I don't know," I said, stepping closer to the door. "But it looks like it's the source of the chaos."

Dana's gaze narrowed in concentration. "We need to get through it. Whatever's happening, it's coming from beyond that door."

I reached out, my hand hovering inches from the door's surface. As soon as I touched it, a jolt of energy surged through my fingers, causing me to pull back with a gasp. My hand felt like it had been seared by hot iron.

"It's a magical ward," I said, shaking my hand to ease the pain. "We can't just walk through it."

Dana's expression hardened with determination. "Then we'll break it."

She moved to the door, her focus narrowing as she began to channel her magic. Her hands glowed with a fierce, blue light as she concentrated on breaking the ward. I watched with bated breath, hoping her magic would be enough to overcome the barrier.

There was a moment of intense energy as Dana's spell collided with the ward, and then—an explosion of light. The red glow flickered violently before dissipating, and the door creaked open.

"Go!" Dana said, her voice strained from the effort.

I followed her through the now-unlocked door, our hearts pounding with every step. The hallway beyond was eerily quiet, the chaos momentarily stilled. We hurried forward, adrenaline surging as we searched for any sign of Jake or Nathaniel.

"Stay alert," Dana murmured, her eyes scanning the corridor. "We don't know what we're walking into."

We moved cautiously down the hall. The silence only added to our anxiety. The distant sound of footsteps grew louder, and I could feel the tension mounting with each step. As we approached a corner, Dana suddenly stopped, holding up a hand.

"Listen," she whispered.

I strained my ears and heard the unmistakable sound of footsteps—several pairs, moving with purpose. Dana and I exchanged worried glances, realizing that we were not alone.

"Get down!" Dana hissed, pulling me behind a nearby table that had been overturned and partially destroyed.

We crouched low, trying to make ourselves as inconspicuous as possible. The footsteps grew closer, the sound of shoes scraping against the floor echoing in the tense silence. I could barely breathe, my heart racing as I listened to the approaching danger.

From our hidden vantage point, I could see shadows moving past us. The figures were too blurred to make out clearly, but they moved with an air of authority and menace.

The footsteps stopped just outside the room, and I held my breath, praying that they wouldn't discover us. The minutes felt like hours as the figures remained outside, their presence a looming threat.

As the footsteps continued to linger, the uncertainty of our situation became almost unbearable. We were caught in a web of chaos and danger, with no clear path forward. The sound of the footsteps was our only clue to the unknown peril that awaited us.

In the darkness beneath the table, I felt a

sense of dread creeping over me. We had managed to evade immediate danger, but the uncertainty of what lay ahead was palpable. With every passing second, the tension mounted, leaving us on the edge of our seats.

The footsteps grew louder once more, and I braced myself for whatever was coming next. The danger was far from over, and my anxiety had never been higher. As I clutched Dana's hand tightly, I could only hope that we would find a way to navigate this perilous situation and emerge unscathed.

And so, we waited, the echoes of impending danger growing louder with each passing moment, as the world outside continued to unravel.

CHAPTER THIRTEEN

The footsteps drew closer, sending shivers down my spine. Dana and I huddled beneath the overturned table, our breaths shallow as we strained to hear any indication of who—or what—was approaching. The tension was almost unbearable. Then, as if the situation wasn't already dire enough, a familiar voice echoed through the hall, cutting through the silence like a knife.

"Come on out, Paige. There's no need to hide."

Prentiss. His voice was smooth, tainted with a cold, unsettling calm. I could almost see his smirk, the same malevolent grin that had haunted my nightmares. He was close, and my heart pounded against my ribs as the reality of our predicament set in.

"Prentiss," Dana whispered, her voice trembling with a mix of fear and anger. "He's here."

Before I could respond, the sound of heavy footsteps halted just outside our hiding spot. Prentiss's voice continued; his tone deceptively soothing. "I assure you; I have no intention of harming either of you. All I want is Paige."

I exchanged a worried glance with Dana. "What does he want from me?" I murmured.

"Don't know," Dana replied, her eyes narrowing. "But we can't just wait here and let him get away with whatever he's planning."

"Paige," Prentiss's voice came again, this time tinged with impatience. "Come out, and let's discuss this rationally. I promise, you won't be harmed."

The sound of the door creaking open followed by a shuffling of feet confirmed that someone had entered the room. I took a deep breath, my mind racing. If I stayed hidden, there was a chance we could be discovered. But if I came out, what was to stop him from capturing us both?

"Stay here," I whispered to Dana. "I'll go out and try to buy us some time. We need to figure out what he wants and how to get out of this."

Dana's hand squeezed mine, her expression one of terror. "Be careful, Paige."

With a deep breath, I steeled myself and crawled out from under the table, emerging into the dim light of the hallway. Prentiss stood there, his tall accomplice looming beside him, a predatory glint in his eyes.

"Hello, Paige," Prentiss said, his voice as smooth as silk. "I'm glad you could join us."

I took a cautious step forward, trying to gauge the situation. "What do you want from me?"

Prentiss's eyes gleamed with a twisted satisfaction. "You see, Paige, I need you to use the device to travel back in time. There's something that must be set right—an unfortunate mistake on your mother's part."

My heart skipped a beat. "My mother? What does she have to do with any of this?"

"The device you're so desperate to protect," Prentiss continued, gesturing toward the glowing, magical object in the tall man's possession, "can take you to any point in time. I need you to go back and prevent your mother from killing me."

I swallowed hard, struggling to process his words. "Why would she kill you?"

Prentiss's smile widened. "That's a story for another time. For now, you have a choice to make. Use the device to change history, or face the consequences."

I felt a surge of anger and fear. "You're insane if you think I'm going to help you."

"Ah, but you see," Prentiss said, "you don't have much choice in the matter. Either you help me, or I ensure you never see the light of day again."

Before I could react, the tall man lunged at me, his dark magic crackling with malevolent energy. I barely had time to raise a defensive shield as the attack collided with my barrier, the force of the blast pushing me back.

"Dana!" I shouted, turning to see her emerging from the hiding spot. She was already casting a powerful spell, her hands glowing with an intense blue light. The energy surged toward Prentiss and his accomplice, creating a barrier of protection between us.

The hallway erupted into chaos. Spells flew in all directions, each burst of magic colliding with opposing forces. I fought to keep my footing, ducking and weaving through the onslaught of energy. The air was thick with the smell of ozone and the sounds of battle—crashing spells, shouts, and the unmistakable crackle of magical forces.

Dana and I worked in tandem, her spells complimenting my own defensive magic. We pushed back against Prentiss and the tall man, our combined efforts slowing their advance. But despite our best efforts, it was clear that we were on the defensive.

"Paige!" Dana called out; her voice strained. "We need to get out of here!"

I glanced around, desperate for a way out. The hallway was a war zone, and the chaos showed no signs of letting up. We had to find an escape route, and fast.

As I fought back against another surge of dark magic, I spotted a door at the far end of the hallway, partially covered by debris. "This way!" I shouted, grabbing Dana's arm and pulling her toward the door.

We raced down the hallway, our footsteps echoing through the destruction. Behind us, Prentiss and the tall man were closing in, their relentless pursuit a constant threat. I could hear their shouts, their magical attacks continuing to bombard us.

We reached the door, and Dana quickly used her magic to force it open. Beyond it lay a narrow passage leading to the back of the building. With no time to lose, we sprinted down the passage, the sounds of the battle growing fainter as we moved further away.

Finally, we emerged into the woods behind the academy, the cool night air a welcome relief from the stifling chaos. But our respite was short-lived. As we stumbled through the trees, a shimmering portal appeared before us, pulsating with a strange, ethereal light.

"What is that?" Dana gasped; her eyes wide with shock.

"It's a portal," I said, my heart pounding. "We need to go through it. It's our only chance."

Without hesitation, we plunged into the portal. The world around us dissolved into a whirl of color and light. The sensation was disorienting, a dizzying blur of time and space. As we hurtled through the portal, I could only hope that it would lead us to safety.

The world reformed around us, and we found ourselves in a new location, our surroundings unfamiliar and alien. I glanced around, trying to get my bearings, but the only certainty was that we had left the immediate danger behind. For now, we were safe from Prentiss and his malevolent schemes. *But what kind of place is this* I thought as we moved hesitantly in silence. What year is it?

Continue the Academy with Paige. Pre-Order Book 4
https://books2read.com/u/3RjwvB

ALSO BY R.L. WILSON

Urban Fantasy

The Urban Fae Series

Eternal Love. https://dl.bookfunnel.com/loqjdqjg40

Eternal Curse. https://books2read.com/u/mowoVW

Eternal Fire. https://books2read.com/u/49l68w

Eternal Shadows https://books2read.com/u/b5kJOp

Eternal Darkness https://books2read.com/u/b5kROA

Paranormal Romance Series

The Omen Club

Dragon Burn. https://books2read.com/u/bWrQQq

Dragon Love https://books2read.com/u/47NxLa

Dragon Curse https://books2read.com/u/mgg2kz

Dragon Flame. https://books2read.com/u/mggQjD

Witch Academy of Ash

Phantom light. https://books2read.com/u/38ewow

Shadow light. https://books2read.com/u/3LneV7

Monster light. https://books2read.com/u/meKBnA

The Magical Jinn Series

Celena's Pack Book 1. https://books2read.com/u/mgPq9K

Celena's Pack Book 2. https://books2read.com/u/bzKlPG

Celena's Pack Book3 https://books2read.com/u/bwylWe

Celenas's Pack Book 4

Celena's Pack Book 5

Misfit Academy

Semester One https://books2read.com/u/47gkGq

Semester Two. https://books2read.com/u/mqexEZ

Semester Three

Urban Fantasy

Moon Hunters Supernatural Agency

Missing Blood https://books2read.com/u/38WNAB

Coming Soon

Supernatural Academy

ABOUT THE AUTHOR

R.L. Wilson is an emerging author of Urban Fantasy/ PNR.

Growing up watching Buffy the vampire slayer and ghost busters, R.L. Wilson became infatuated with the paranormal world.

When she is not writing or plotting her next book she enjoys spending time with her family and her cute cat.

STALK ME

Follow me on social media

FB: facebook.com/rlwilson723

Twitter: twitter.com/exquisitenovel1

Instagram: instagram.com/rlwilson23

Tik Tok: https://vm.tiktok.com/ZMJnQnPgY/"

Join my reader group https://www.facebook.com/groups/440691789814122/

Sign-up for my newsletter and claim a free book. https://dl.bookfunnel.com/l0qjdqjg4o

Check out my website
www.rlwilsonauthor.com

Milton Keynes UK
Ingram Content Group UK Ltd.
UKHW020739071024
449371UK00014B/951